D0502792

For my mother, Roberta, who says
hello to everyone. Love you, Mom!

—M.G.

To my dog, Archer, and all the other
pets who have made a difference.

—P.B.

Text copyright © 2017 by Maria Gianferrari
Illustrations copyright © 2017 by Patrice Barton

Published by Roaring Brook Press
Roaring Brook Press is a division of
Holtzbrinck Publishing Holdings Limited Partnership
175 Fifth Avenue, New York, New York 10010

mackids.com

All rights reserved

Library of Congress Cataloging-in-Publication Data

Names: Gianferrari, Maria, author. | Barton, Patrice, 1955– illustrator.
Title: Hello goodbye dog / Maria Gianferrari ; illustrated by Patrice Barton.
Description: New York : Roaring Brook Press, 2017. | Summary: A student who uses a
    wheelchair finds a way to see her dog each day in school.
Identifiers: LCCN 2016038468 | ISBN 9781626721777 (hardback)
Subjects: | CYAC: Dogs—Fiction. | Schools—Fiction. | People with disabilities—Fiction. |
    Wheelchairs—Fiction. | BISAC: JUVENILE FICTION / Animals / Dogs. | JUVENILE FICTION /
    School & Education. | JUVENILE FICTION / Social Issues / Special Needs.
Classification: LCC PZ7.G339028 He 2017 | DDC [E]—dc23
LC record available at https://lccn.loc.gov/2016038468

Our books may be purchased in bulk for promotional, educational, or business use. Please
contact your local bookseller or the Macmillan Corporate and Premium Sales Department at
(800) 221-7945 ext. 5442 or by e-mail at MacmillanSpecialMarkets@macmillan.com.

First edition, 2017
Book design by Kristie Radwilowicz
Printed in the United States of America by Worzalla,
Stevens Point, Wisconsin

3 5 7 9 10 8 6 4 2

Hello Goodbye
Dog

WRITTEN BY
Maria Gianferrari

ILLUSTRATED BY
Patrice Barton

ROARING BROOK PRESS

NEW YORK

H ello, Moose!" said Zara.
There was nothing Moose loved more
than hello.

Hello was a ride in the car.

"Goodbye, Moose," said Zara. "It's time for school."
Moose put on her brakes.
It took Mom
and Dad
to get Moose to leave.

There was nothing Moose disliked more than goodbye.
Goodbye was an itch that couldn't be scratched.

When Mom checked the mailbox, out zoomed Moose.
It was time to say, "Hello!"

Two paws padded on the glass.

"Oh, my!" said Mrs. Perkins.

"It's my dog, Moose," said Zara.

"Hello, Moose!" said the class.

Hello was a pat on the head.

"Dogs aren't allowed in school," said Mrs. Perkins.

"Moose will be quiet," said Zara. "She loves story time."

Moose lay at Zara's feet as Mrs.
Perkins read a story.

"Goodbye, Moose," said Zara.
Moose put on her brakes.
It took Mom,
Dad,
Zara,
and Mrs. Perkins
to get Moose to leave.

Goodbye was being tied up in the backyard.

Moose chewed through the rope. It was time to say, "Hello!"

"Hello, Moose!" cried Zara.

Hello was having a book and someone to read it to you.

"Dogs aren't allowed in the library," said Ms. Chen.

"Moose will be quiet," said Zara. "She likes when I read to her."

Zara read.

Kids listened.

Moose's tail swept circles on the rug.

"Goodbye, Moose," said Zara.
Moose put on her brakes.

It took Mom,
Dad,
Zara,
Mrs. Perkins,
and Ms. Chen
to get Moose to leave.

Goodbye was a closing door.

Moose pushed through the screen.
It was time to say, "Hello!"

"Hello, Moose!" said Zara.
Hello smelled like homemade cookies.

"Dogs aren't allowed in the cafeteria,"
said one of the lunch ladies.

"She'll be quiet—I'll just read to her,"
said Zara.

Zara read.

One kid sat.

Then another.

And another, until the table was full.

Moose's tail thumped on the floor.

"What's that dog doing here?"
asked Principal Evans.

"It's time for goodbye, Moose,"
said Zara.

But Moose was tired of goodbye.
A game of tag was on.
Principal Evans was "It."

Chairs tipped.
Kids slipped.
Teachers tripped.
Trays flipped.
And Moose skipped—
right back to Zara.

Then Moose got tagged.

"Goodbye, Moose," said Zara.

It took Mom,
Dad,
Zara,
Mrs. Perkins,
Ms. Chen,
Principal Evans,
and all the lunch ladies
to get Moose to leave.

Goodbye was tag without an "It."

Goodbye was tug and no war.

Goodbye was hide without seek.

Goodbye was being alone.

AAAA-WO

"*AAAA-WOOO*," yowled Moose.
She needed to say, "Hello,"
but Zara wasn't there.

"Hello, Moose," said Zara. "I know you
don't like goodbyes, and I have an idea!"

Zara took Moose to
therapy dog school.

Moose was tested . . .

On her temperament.

✓ Check.

On sitting. Lying
down. Staying.

✓ Check.

On being with children.

Check.

On being around wheelchairs.

Double check.

Finally, Moose was ready.

The next day, Moose joined Zara in the classroom.

"Hello, Moose!" said the class,

Mrs. Perkins,

Ms. Chen,

Principal Evans,

and all the lunch ladies.

Today was hello.

Author's Note

Dogs can be bridges between people who might never talk to one another. Dogs can bring people closer together. But most of all, dogs provide us with unconditional love. And therapy dogs just happen to be experts in giving unconditional love. They differ from service dogs in that they do not undergo such extensive training. Therapy dogs are tested and evaluated for reliability, calmness, and their ability to give affection. Their main function is to provide emotional support in a variety of environments, from classrooms to hospitals, nursing homes, and even correctional facilities.

Therapy dogs can be used in classrooms and libraries to foster a love of reading. Therapy reading dogs provide a "pawsitive" association with reading, and especially with reading aloud, since child readers are neither judged on nor corrected for mispronunciation. Instead, they read for the sheer enjoyment of their audience—a dog. Who wags her tail? Who gives you his rapt attention? Who listens, even if the story is boring? Who rests her head on your ankles? A dog. It's the perfect combination: tales and tails!

For more information on dogs as classroom readers and to find therapy reading dog programs near you, consult the following websites:

Librarydogs: librarydogs.com

Therapy Dogs International: tdi-dog.org

PHOTOGRAPHS COURTESY OF WHITTIER PUBLIC LIBRARY (WHITTIER, CALIFORNIA)

31901060747385